I AM READING

VIVIAN FRENCH

ILLUSTRATED BY

CLIVE SCRUTON

KINGFISHER
BOSTON

For all the lovely people at the Windsor Lodge Hotel—V. F.
For my nan, the best mince pie maker—C. S.

KINGFISHER
a Houghton Mifflin Company imprint
222 Berkeley Street
Boston, Massachusetts 02116
www.houghtonmifflinbooks.com

First published by Kingfisher in 1999
This edition published in 2004
4 6 8 10 9 7 5 3
3TR/0506/WKT/GRS(GRS)/115MA

LIBRARY OF CONGRESS CATALOGING–IN–PUBLICATION DATA
Mrs. Hippo's Pizza Parlor/by Vivian French; illustrated by Clive Scruton—1st ed.
p. cm.—I am reading
Summary: Business is bad at Mrs. Hippo's Pizza Parlor until her son William has a
brilliant idea.
[1. Pizza—Fiction. 2. Hippopotamus—Fiction. 3. Animals—Fiction.] I. Scruton,Clive, ill.
II. Title. III. Series.
SP7.F88917 Mr 2000
[Fic}—dc21   99-054153

ISBN 0-7534-5823-3

Printed in China

Contents

Chapter One

It was two o'clock in the afternoon.

Mrs. Hippo's Pizza Parlor

was empty.

Mrs. Hippo was asleep.

William Hippo was reading

his comic book. It was very quiet.

No one wanted to buy a pizza.

William put down his comic book

and scratched his head.

He liked pizza.

His friends loved pizza.

So why didn't they come to

Mrs. Hippo's Pizza Parlor?

Were they going somewhere

else instead?

Big Pig's Burger Bar gave away balloons.

Big Pig's Burger Bar had posters
all over town.

Maybe everyone was going there.

William's ears drooped.

If no one came to buy pizza,

there'd be no money.

No money meant no shopping . . .

and no shopping meant no bicycle

for William's birthday.

He'd seen a bicycle in the bicycle store.

It was bright green with a big bell.

William wanted that green bicycle.

He wanted it very badly.

RING!

It was the doorbell.

William ran to open the door.

"Hello!" said Ellie Bear.

"I've come to play!"

"Have you?" said William. "Why?"

Mrs. Hippo opened one eye.

"Mother Bear's busy," she said.

"Come in, Ellie dear."

Ellie Bear took off her coat.

"May I have a drink?" she asked.

William looked hopeful.

"Can we have brownies, too?" he said.

"Two brownies each," said Mrs. Hippo.

"I haven't been shopping."

"Why not?" asked Ellie.

William leaned toward Ellie.

"No one comes to buy pizza anymore," he whispered, "so we don't have any money."

Mrs. Hippo made hot chocolate

for Ellie and William.

She put four brownies on a plate.

"Here you are, dearies," she said.

Then she went to make

herself a cup of tea.

Ellie drank her hot chocolate
very fast.

"I'm going to dunk my brownies
in your hot chocolate," she told William.
She leaned over the table . . .

William's hot chocolate spilled
everywhere.

"Oops!" said Ellie. "Sorry!"

William went to get a cloth.

When William came back, the plate

was empty.

William put down the cloth with a

SPLATTT!

"Mom!" he yelled. "MOM!"

12

Mrs. Hippo came hurrying in.

"What's the matter?" she asked.

"Ellie ate ALL the brownies!"
said William.

Mrs. Hippo looked at the mess.

"I think it's time we went out,"
she said.

"Let's go to the beach."

"YES!" shouted Ellie and
William together.

Chapter Two

Behind the pizza parlor

was a little yard.

In the yard was a motorcycle.

A gleaming, glittering motorcycle . . .

with a bright red sidecar.

The wheels were shiny silver.

The handlebars were wide.

The horn was LOUD.

"WOW!" said Ellie.

"That's MUCH better than a bicycle!"

William didn't answer.

He wanted a bright green bicycle

that he could ride by himself.

"Helmets on!" said Mrs. Hippo.

"And hop inside!

BRRRRRRRRMMM!

Mrs. Hippo revved up the motorcycle.

"Hooray!" shouted Ellie.

"Go for it, Mom!" shouted William.

BRRRRRRRRRRRMMM!

They were off!

Down the road went the motorcycle.

VROOM! VROOM!

They waved to little Tilly Tiger

and her dad at the bus stop.

Under the bridge.

VROOM! VROOM!

They waved to the giraffe family
on their tricycles.

Right at the gas station.

VROOM! VROOM!

They waved to the
monkey mechanics.

Left at the supermarket.

VROOM! VROOM!

They waved to Auntie Elephant.

Auntie Elephant was having

too much trouble with her

shopping cart to wave back.

They zoomed on down to the beach.

"WHEEEEEEEEEEEEEEE!!"

yelled Ellie and William.

Mrs. Hippo roared along the

road to the beach.

She roared over the boardwalk

and down to the sand.

Then she stopped.

"WOW!" said Ellie as she got out.

"That was FUN!"

Chapter Three

"Now," said Mrs. Hippo.

"How about building a sand castle?"

"NO!" said Ellie. "I want to go for another ride!"

"Me, too," said William.

Ellie looked at the smooth, yellow sand.

"Can we ride on the sand?"

she asked.

"Well . . ." said Mrs. Hippo.

"There's no one here," said Ellie.

"We could make tracks!" said William.

Ellie jumped up. "We could write
ELLIE in the sand!"

"YES!" William jumped up too.

"EVERYONE will see it!" said Ellie.

"They'll see it on the moon!"

Ellie and William rushed back
into the sidecar.

Mrs. Hippo climbed onto the
motorcycle.

BRRRRRRRRRRRMMM!

They were off.

First of all they wrote ELLIE

in the sand.

"That's good," said Ellie. "Now

write William."

"No," said William.

"Why not?" asked Ellie.

"I have an idea," William said.

His eyes were shining.

"An idea about the pizza parlor!

It's a MUCH better idea than

Big Pig's posters!"

He whispered in Mrs. Hippo's ear.

Mrs. Hippo nodded . . .

"Write it BIG, Mom," William told her.

Mrs. Hippo got ready.

BRRRRRRRRRRRRMMM!!

They roared right across the sand.

Up and down

and around and around.

At last Mrs. Hippo stopped.

They all looked at the sand.

"WOW!" said Ellie.

"'MRS. HIPPO'S PIZZA IS
THE BEST!'"

"EVERYONE will see that!" William
said happily. "They won't want to go
to Big Pig's Burger Bar now."

"They'll see it forever and ever!"
said Ellie.

"No, dearie," said Mrs. Hippo.

"The tide will come in tonight.

It will wash the sand all clean and

smooth again."

"Oh," said Ellie. Then she smiled.

"We could do it again tomorrow!"

"Maybe," said Mrs. Hippo.

"But now we'd better be going home."

"Can we have some ice cream?"

asked Ellie.

Mrs. Hippo shook her head.

"I'm sorry, dearie," she said.

"Look! Not even a penny in my purse!"

William looked sad again.

He thought about his birthday.

They'd have to sell lots and LOTS
of pizza to make enough money for
a green bicycle.

A bright green bicycle with a big bell.

"What's the matter, William?"
asked Ellie.

"Nothing," said William.

"We'll go home the long way,"
said Mrs. Hippo. "That'll cheer us all up!"

Chapter Four

It was five o'clock when they
got home.

"Mom!" said William.

"Look at all those people outside
our pizza parlor!"

"Dear me," said Mrs. Hippo.

"I think they're waiting to come in!"

"What do they want?" asked Ellie.

"PIZZA!" said William.

"HOORAY!"

They all hurried inside.

"Come on, Ellie!" said William.

"We've got things to do!"

"I'll help," said Ellie. "I like helping!"

Mrs. Hippo turned on the oven.

Then she grated the cheese . . .

and cut up the onions . . .

and sliced the mushrooms . . .

and diced the peppers.

William rolled out the pizza dough.

And Ellie helped too.

She cleaned up the tables . . .

and swept the floor . . .

and shook the ketchup bottle . . .

"Ellie," said Mrs. Hippo.

"Yes?" said Ellie.

Mrs. Hippo took away the ketchup bottle.

"Wouldn't you like to read William's
comic book?"

"No," said Ellie. "I like helping."

At five-thirty Mrs. Hippo opened
the pizza parlor door.
"Please come in," she said.
"We saw your sign on the sand,"
said Tilly Tiger.
"So did I!" said Auntie Elephant.

"We did too!" said Grandpa Giraffe.

"Don't want burgers anymore!"
said Baby Giraffe.

"We love pizza!" said the monkeys.

"That's right!" everybody said.

"We LOVE pizza!!"

Mrs. Hippo and William
worked and worked.
Ellie went on helping.

At seven-thirty Mother Bear came into
the pizza parlor.

"Oh my!" she said. "You ARE busy!"

"Yes," puffed Mrs. Hippo, "we are!"

Ellie gave her mother a big hug.

"We wrote, 'Mrs. Hippo's Pizza
is the Best!' in the sand, and now
everybody's coming to try it!"

"YES!" said Willliam. "And they all want LOTS and LOTS of pizza!"

Mrs. Hippo nodded. "Tomorrow I'm cooking a new Seaside Special— so they're all going to come back and bring their friends!"

"Goodness!" said Mother Bear.

"We'd love to see Ellie again,"
said Mrs. Hippo. "What about Sunday?"
"That's my birthday!" said William.
"That's right," said Mrs. Hippo.
"Ellie can come for your birthday
and see your present!"
And she winked at Ellie and gave
William a big hug.

Chapter Five

On Sunday Ellie rang the doorbell.

RING!

William opened the door.

"Hi!" said Ellie. "Where's your

present from your mom?"

"Come and see," said William.

And there in the middle of the

pizza parlor was . . .

the bright green bicycle with a big bell.

And what did they have to eat?

SPECIAL BIRTHDAY PIZZA!!!

About the author and illustrator

Vivian French used to be an actor. She has written many books for children and often visits schools and libraries to tell her stories. She and Clive Scruton have been friends for a long time. They first thought up the story of *Mrs. Hippo's Pizza Parlor* while sitting together on a beach . . . eating pizza!

Clive Scruton wanted to be either Spider-Man or an astronaut when he was a child. But then he discovered he could draw—and has since illustrated more than 50 books for children. Now he is married and lives in a house surrounded by his children, their rabbits, and his own comic books and robots. Clive often goes on bicycle rides . . . but what he really wants is a bright red motorcycle with a sidecar!

Strategies for Independent Readers

Predict
Think about the cover, illustrations, and the title of the book. What do you think this book will be about? While you are reading think about what may happen next and why.

Monitor
As you read ask yourself if what you're reading makes sense. If it doesn't, reread, look at the illustrations, or read ahead.

Question
Ask yourself questions about important ideas in the story such as what the characters might do or what you might learn.

Phonics
If there is a word that you do not know, look carefully at the letters, sounds, and word parts that you do know. Blend the sounds to read the word. Ask yourself if this is a word you know. Does it make sense in the sentence?

Summarize
Think about the characters, the setting where the story takes place, and the problem the characters faced in the story. Tell the important ideas in the beginning, middle, and end of the story.

Evaluate
Ask yourself questions like: Did you like the story? Why or why not? How did the author make the story come alive? How did the author make the story fun to read? How well did you understand the story? Maybe you can understand it better if you read it again!